Animals That Sting

Written by Claire Saxby

Photography by Gary Lewis

alphakids

Introduction

Many animals sting.

Some animals sting to get food.
Others sting when they are in danger.

Some animals do both.

Mosquitoes

Mosquitoes are looking for food
when they sting you.

Mosquitoes don't bite with teeth.
They suck blood through their long,
thin mouths.

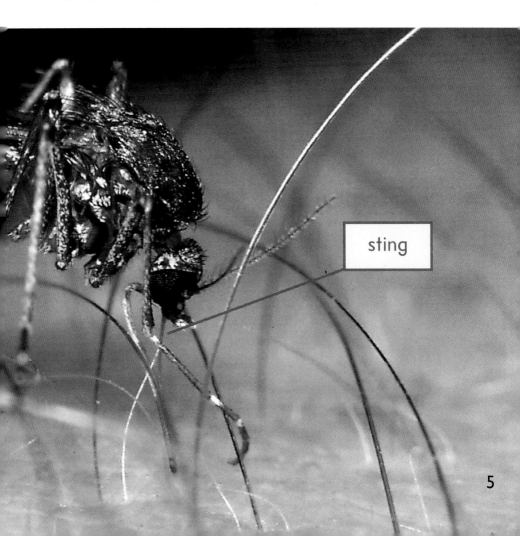

sting

Caterpillars

Some caterpillars have hairs that sting.
Poison comes out when a hair is touched.

These hairs stop animals from eating the
caterpillars.

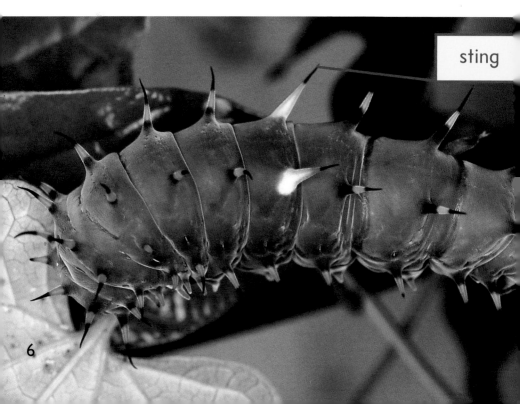

sting

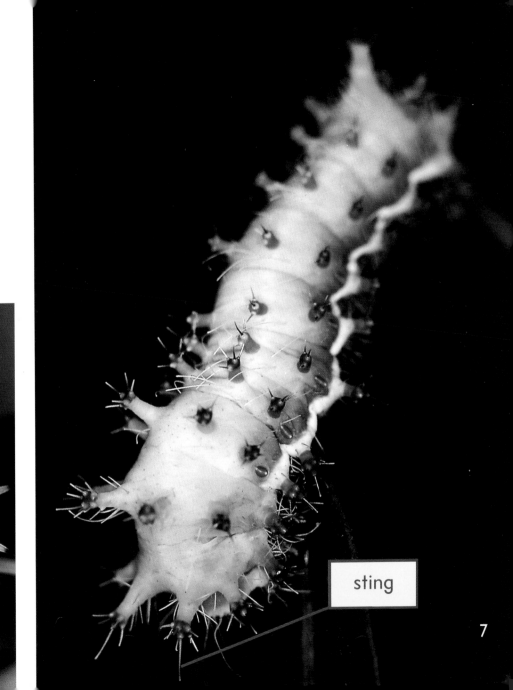

sting

Scorpions

Scorpions have poison in the tips of their tails. They bend their tails over their heads when they sting.

Scorpions use their sting to kill food. They also sting when they are in danger.

sting

Jellyfish

Jellyfish have tentacles with small, poisonous stings.

Jellyfish shoot these stings to kill their food.

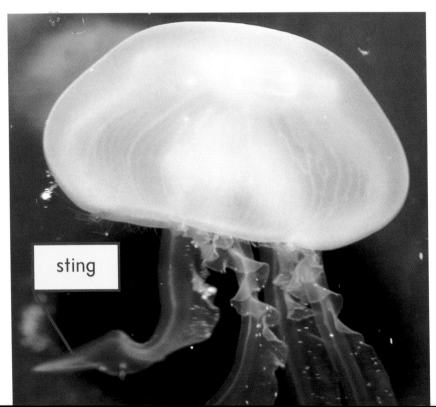

sting

sting

Stingrays

Stingrays have long, thin tails with stinging spines.
They have poison at the bottom of each spine.

sting

Stingrays use their tails like
a whip when they are attacked.

Bees and wasps

Bees and wasps have a sting on the end of their bodies.
A poison sac is at the end of the sting.

Bees sting once and then they die.
Wasps can sting many times.

sting

Conclusion

There are many ways that animals can sting.

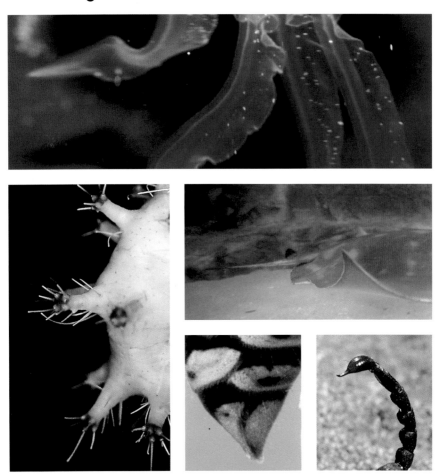